The Books About Molly

★

Meet Molly · An American Girl

While her father is fighting in World War Two, Molly and her brother start their own war at home.

★

Molly Learns a Lesson · A School Story

Molly and her friends plan a secret project to help the war effort, and learn about allies and cooperation.

★

Molly's Surprise · A Christmas Story

Molly makes plans for Christmas surprises, but she ends up being surprised herself.

★

Happy Birthday, Molly! · A Springtime Story

An English girl comes to stay with Molly, but she's not what Molly expects!

★

Molly Saves the Day · A Summer Story

At summer camp, Molly has to pretend to be her friend's enemy and face her own fears, too.

★

Changes for Molly · A Winter Story

Dad will return from the war any day! Will he arrive in time to see the "grown up" Molly perform as Miss Victory?

MOLLY
LEARNS
A LESSON
A SCHOOL STORY

BY VALERIE TRIPP

ILLUSTRATIONS NICK BACKES

VIGNETTES KEITH SKEEN, RENÉE GRAEF

PLEASANT COMPANY

Published by Pleasant Company Publications
© Copyright 1986, 1989 by Pleasant Company
For information, address: Book Editor,
Pleasant Company Publications,
8400 Fairway Place, P.O. Box 620998,
Middleton, WI 53562.

First Edition.
Printed in the United States of America.
97 98 99 RND 29 28

The American Girls Collection® and Molly McIntire®
are registered trademarks of Pleasant Company.

PICTURE CREDITS
The following individuals and organizations have generously given
permission to reprint illustrations contained in "Looking Back":
pp. 62-63–Courtesy Library of Congress; Courtesy Library of Congress;
Courtesy Library of Congress; pp. 64-65–UPI/Bettmann Newsphotos,
Courtesy LIFE Picture Service; Courtesy Library of Congress; AP/Wide
World Photos; AP/ Wide World Photos; John W. Lewis; pp. 66-67–Beverly
Stevens; Ernest E. Cole.

Edited by Jeanne Thieme
Designed by Myland McRevey

Library of Congress Cataloging-in-Publication Data

Tripp, Valerie, 1951–
Molly learns a lesson: a school story
by Valerie Tripp; illustrations, Nick Backes; vignettes, Keith Skeen, Renée Graef.

p.cm.–(The American girls collection)
Summary: During World War II, nine-year-old Molly
goes to school and with her friends tries to aid the war effort.
[1. Schools–Fiction.   2. World War, 1939-1945–United States–Fiction.]
I. Backes, Nick, ill.   II. Title.   III. Series.
PZ7.T7363Mo 1990   [Fic]–dc19   89-3906   CIP   AC
ISBN 0-937295-84-1   ISBN 0-937295-16-7 (pbk.)

TO ALL
MY TEACHERS

TABLE OF CONTENTS

MOLLY'S FAMILY
AND FRIENDS

MOLLY'S FAMILY

MOLLY

A nine-year-old who is growing up on the home front in America during World War Two.

DAD

Molly's father, a doctor who is somewhere in England, taking care of wounded soldiers.

MOM

Molly's mother, who holds the family together while Dad is away.

JILL

Molly's fourteen-year-old sister, who is always trying to act grown-up.

RICKY

Molly's twelve-year-old brother—a big pest.

BRAD

Molly's five-year-old brother—a little pest.

LINDA

One of Molly's best friends, a practical schemer.

SUSAN

Molly's other best friend, a cheerful dreamer.

MRS. GILFORD

The housekeeper, who rules the roost when Mom is at work.

MISS CAMPBELL

Molly's teacher, who keeps her third-graders on their toes.

ALISON

One of Molly's friends from school.

EIGHT TIMES SEVEN

Molly McIntire loved to look at her teacher, Miss Campbell. Miss Campbell's hair was brown and so smooth and shiny it reminded Molly of dark, polished wood. Most of the time Miss Campbell wore her hair pinned on top of her head in a soft roll. But sometimes, like today, she wore it down in a page boy. Her long, glossy curls just brushed her shoulders and swung like a dancer's skirt when she turned her head quickly. Molly touched the ends of her own hair. *Sticks,* she thought. *My hair is as straight as sticks.* When Molly grew up, she wanted her hair to look just like Miss Campbell's, but it had a long way to go.

Today Miss Campbell was wearing a bright red sweater exactly the color of six red geraniums that stood saluting the sun on the windowsill. Miss Campbell sat up straight on the piano stool and sang along with the class in a clear, firm voice:

"America, America!
God shed His grace on thee.
And crown thy good with brotherhood
From sea to shining sea!"

Then she smiled at the class. "Excellent! Now let's get to work. We have a great deal to do today."

Molly watched Miss Campbell write "Things to

Do Today" on the blackboard. When some teachers wrote that, it looked like a scold or the heading to a long list of tiresome tasks. But when Miss Campbell wrote it, in round even letters, it looked like a challenge. Wake up! Sharpen your pencils! The day is beginning! Miss Campbell expected her third-graders to be on their toes. She often said, "School is your war duty. Being a good student is as important as being a good soldier."

Miss Campbell wrote

Howie Munson began waving his hand wildly, as if he were drowning at sea and Miss Campbell were the rescue ship.

"Yes, Howard?" Miss Campbell said.

Howie stood up next to his desk. "Miss Campbell, ma'am, don't forget, yesterday you said we could have a multiplication bee."

Molly groaned to herself. Howie said "multiplication bee" as if it would be a big treat, like cupcakes for lunch. Molly absolutely hated multiplication bees. They made her so nervous she forgot problems she knew by heart, even the easy ones like two times two. She hid her hands in her lap and crossed her fingers. *Please let her say no,* she prayed.

But Miss Campbell was laughing. "You're right, Howard. We will have a multiplication contest today. I have a big gold badge for the student who wins the contest, too!"

"I bet it will be me, Miss Campbell," said Howie. "I know 'em all! Just ask me anything!"

"We'll see, Howard," said Miss Campbell. "But right now, please be seated."

Howie sat down at his desk. He was so excited he raised his clenched fists above his head like a prize fighter. "Howard," said Miss Campbell firmly, "please save your celebration until after the contest."

Howie sat right behind Molly. There were twenty-one students in Molly's class, ten girls and eleven boys. They were seated in alphabetical order at desks arranged in four straight rows. Molly sat at the middle desk in the third row, in back of Grace Littlefield, the new girl who was as quiet as a

4

mouse. Molly's two best friends, Linda and Susan, were also in Miss Campbell's class.

The classroom was large and square, smelling of chalk dust, books, and turtle food. It was painted pale green, with a high ceiling and a shiny wooden floor. Along one wall, above the bookshelves, there were windows. They were tall windows, twice as tall as Molly. It was quite a job to open them at the top. You had to pull them down with a long pole that had a metal knob at the end. It was tricky to fit the knob into the hole all the way at the top of the window, and you had to be strong because the pole was heavy. Then you had to pull on it with all your weight to make the window open even a crack. Being asked to open the top windows was an honor which Miss Campbell gave to everyone in turn. It

didn't matter how big you were, or how well you had managed the job in the past. Everyone got a chance, fair and square. Her fairness was one of the things everyone liked most about Miss Campbell.

Miss Campbell's desk was in the front of the room, right under the flag.

But she hardly ever sat at it. She walked around the room as she talked, or stood by the bookshelves, the blackboard, the piano, or a student's desk. Molly loved it when Miss Campbell stopped at her desk. She smelled like peppermints. Up close, her hands were smooth, square, and small. They were very neat and tidy, just like Miss Campbell. When Miss Campbell explained things—like nouns and verbs, and when *i* comes before *e*—she made them seem neat and tidy, too. With Miss Campbell leading the way, the school day marched along smoothly from the first song of the day to the last dismissal bell.

Right now, Miss Campbell was standing in the front of the room by the maps. The maps were rolled up on poles like window shades. Molly loved it when Miss Campbell pulled down one of the

maps. The sun would catch a ring on her hand and send rainbows of light dancing on the walls. Susan, Linda, and Molly spent a lot of time discussing that ring. Susan thought it was an engagement ring and that Miss Campbell was engaged to marry a soldier who was off fighting the

war. Linda said nobody knew for sure if that was true or not. Molly hoped very much that it was. She hoped that Miss Campbell's soldier would come home soon and Miss Campbell would ask Molly to be the flower girl in her wedding. Molly would carry a little basket of flower petals, or maybe she'd hold the train of Miss Campbell's wedding dress. Any day now, Miss Campbell would come to her and ask, "Molly? . . ."

"Molly?"

Molly sat up straight at her desk. Miss Campbell *was* asking her something, but it wasn't about flower petals. "Molly, your mind is a million miles away. Perhaps while you're bringing it back to our classroom, someone else can tell us the name of the capital city of England. Grace, can you help us?"

"London!" squeaked Grace, proud to know the answer.

Hmph! thought Molly. *Everybody knows that.*

"That's right, Grace," Miss Campbell said. On the map, she pointed to London with her long, rubber-tipped pointer. "And who can tell me why it's important for us to know about England and London?"

Molly shot her hand up before anyone else.

"Molly?"

Molly stood next to her desk to answer. "Because of the war. America and England are fighting together in the war against Germany. We're helping England. I know because my father's there working in a hospital. The Germans are bombing England, and my father is taking care of the soldiers who get hurt in battles."

Molly stopped talking and sat down. She didn't really like to talk about her father being in England. It made her remember that he was in danger and very, very far away. Sometimes she worried that he might get hurt by a German bomb. She looked at the map. The ocean between America and England looked awfully big. And England looked awfully small, and not very safe. It was so little, in such a big ocean, so near Germany and so far from home.

Miss Campbell smiled at Molly. "Very good, Molly. Thank you for telling the class about your father. You must be very proud of him." She turned to the blackboard. "Molly's right. The

United States and England are *allies*. That means we're working together to beat Germany." Miss Campbell wrote on the board

Allies—People who work together for the same goal.

"America is cooperating with England because we hope we can get the job of winning the war done faster if we help each other," Miss Campbell said. "Now, for next Tuesday, I'd like you to write three paragraphs about cooperation and why it's a good idea for people to work together. Tell how allies can help each other. Remember to indent at the beginning of every new paragraph. Use whole sentences, periods, and capitals."

Woody Halsey raised his hand. "Does spelling count?" he asked.

"Yes, Woody, spelling counts," said Miss Campbell. "Use the dictionary. Be as careful as you can be. And speaking of 'be's,' it's time for the multiplication bee! Line up quietly."

Howie Munson was the first one out of his seat. "Boys against girls!" he blurted out.

"Let's calm down, please, Howard. Boys, line up by the windows. Girls, line up by the door. Woody, there will be no pushing in line, please."

Everyone chattered happily as the teams rushed to line up. Molly walked over to the girls' line and stood on the very end. *Maybe I could step back into the cloakroom and hide,* she thought. *Maybe no one would miss me.*

"Nine times six!" Miss Campbell said, and the race was on.

Molly's stomach felt as if it were full of sloshing water. *Maybe I'll throw up,* she thought.

"Seven times seven!"

"Forty-nine!"

"Four times eight!"

"Thirty-two!"

Hardly anyone waited even a second. Molly wondered how people could slap those answers down so quickly. She leaned against the bulletin board that had a display of the planets on it. *I wish I were on another planet right now,* she thought. *I bet no one on Mars cares about multiplication.*

The girl behind Molly gave her a little shove. "Move up," she said. "You're right after Susan."

"I wish I were on another planet right now,"
Molly thought.

Molly gulped. Susan was next. *Maybe we'll have a fire drill,* Molly thought.

"Fifty-four," said Susan smoothly. All the girls clapped and patted her on the back as she walked to the end of the line.

"Nine times twelve!"

Woody Halsey squinted at the ceiling. "One . . . hundred . . . and . . . eight," he said.

"Okay!" said the other boys. "Good going, Woody!"

Now it was Molly's turn.

"Eight times seven!"

Molly froze. The eights! Her worst! She hated the eights!

"Eight times seven," Miss Campbell repeated.

Molly closed her eyes. *Eight times seven. Eight times seven. Probably in the fifties somewhere,* she thought.

"Uh . . . fifty . . . nine?" Molly offered timidly. She thought she was probably wrong. Sure enough, all the girls groaned. Howie jumped out of line and yelled, "Fifty-six! Fifty-six! Eight times seven is fifty-six!"

"Why, Molly," said Miss Campbell. "I think

you need a little more practice with the multiplication flash cards. You'd better review your eights until you know them."

Molly didn't say anything. She walked to her desk and sat down, stiff with shame. The multiplication contest went on around her. Questions and answers buzzed back and forth across the room like bees to a hive. Molly wanted to put her fingers in her ears to block out the numbers. "Nine times six!" "Thirteen times three!" Nobody else missed a problem for a long time. Then slowly, one by one, others took their seats. Finally, only Howie and Alison were left.

"All right," said Miss Campbell. "One more problem, and whoever answers first is the winner. Ready?"

Alison and Howie nodded.

"Twelve times thirteen."

Howie bit his lip and scowled.

"One hundred fifty-six," said Alison calmly.

"Hurray! We win!" cried all the girls except Molly. They all ran up to Alison to hug her. Everyone except Molly, even the boys, clapped when Miss Campbell pinned a big, shiny gold badge on Alison's sweater. "Excellent work, Alison. I'm proud of you."

Alison beamed. Molly saw her look down at the gold badge and touch it with her fingers. Molly looked away. She pulled her three-ring notebook out of her desk and opened it to a blank piece of paper. In big numbers she wrote

—

LEND A HAND

 The day dragged on forever after the multiplication bee. At lunch, Molly felt as if she had a sore throat. She opened her lunch bag and looked inside. Mrs. Gilford had packed a peanut butter and jelly sandwich. Molly took a bite. It got stuck in her throat. She decided she was probably getting the mumps.

In reading, which was usually Molly's favorite subject, she didn't get a chance to read out loud because Miss Campbell stopped the reading group early. Miss Campbell stood in the front of the room and raised both hands, the signal for quiet. All the rustling and chair squeaks and whispers stopped

when she said, "Class, I have a special announcement to make, if I may have your attention,
please."

Molly looked up. A special announcement? It
was something good, she could tell, because Miss
Campbell's face looked pink and pleased.

"Our class has been invited to participate in a
school-wide contest. It's called the Lend-a-Hand
Contest. Every student is challenged to lend a hand
to help the war effort. Every class will be divided
into teams. You may divide yourself into teams in
any way you wish."

"Boys against girls!" said Howie definitely.
"Boys against girls!" All the boys murmured in
agreement.

Miss Campbell waited for quiet. "Well, that will
be fine if that's the way you want to do it. You may
choose any kind of project you wish, but it must be
something to help our soldiers in the war effort. At
the end of the contest, the winning team will
receive an award at a school assembly. Now, you
have only one weekend to do the project from start
to finish. Plan your projects today. Work on them
tomorrow. Bring them in on Monday. Remember,

you will be competing against boys and girls in the fourth and fifth grades, so be sure you choose a very good project to do, and work hard on it."

The classroom was awash in a sea of voices as the teams discussed different ideas for their projects. Linda waved to Susan while Alison whispered to Grace. Woody sat on top of his desk, talking to Howie over Grace's head. Then Susan leaned over to Molly. "What should we do?" she asked.

"I don't know," said Molly. She tried to think of a spectacular project. Collect a thousand dollars and buy a War Bond? No, too hard. Roll bandages? Too boring. Collect newspapers? Everyone did that. Oh, the third grade girls just *had* to win the contest. Just think how pleased Miss Campbell would be! Molly would work harder than anyone else on the project, and then when they won, she'd have her picture in the newspaper, probably with Miss Campbell. THIRD GRADE GIRL LENDS A BIG HAND TO WAR EFFORT, it would say under the picture. And Miss Campbell would send the picture to the soldier she was engaged to, and he would write back, "Let's ask

Molly McIntire to be in our wedding. . . ."

"What a wonderful idea, Alison!" Miss Campbell was saying. "I think that's a fine project for the third grade girls. You certainly have *your* thinking cap on today."

On the blackboard Miss Campbell wrote

Knit socks! Molly thought. *That's a terrible idea!* Molly knew all about knitting socks. Well, she didn't really know *all* about it, but she knew it was hard. Molly had struggled through knitting lessons with Mrs. Gilford. She had not been able to finish even one sock. Socks took a long time. They were complicated. By the time Mrs. Gilford finished a sock, it looked as if it had already marched a million miles. The third grade girls would never win the contest if they chose knitting socks as a project.

Molly just had to say something. But as she started to raise her hand, Susan leaned over and

18

whispered, "Won't that be fun? We can make hundreds of socks if we all knit this weekend."

Molly brought her hand down. No one would listen to her now. All the other girls were gathered in a bunch around Alison's desk. They decided to unravel old sweaters or ask their mothers for yarn scraps they could use. Alison was smiling and nodding, writing something on a piece of paper.

That Alison! thought Molly. *It would be her idea. Always trying to get in good with Miss Campbell!*

Well, Molly wasn't going to let Alison tell her what to do. She wasn't going to let Alison lead all the girls in the class into some dumb project that wouldn't even work. Molly sat at her desk thinking hard. It wasn't easy to concentrate because all around her the boys were talking loudly about their project. Woody Halsey wanted to dig an air raid shelter for the school. "All's we'd need would be some shovels," he kept saying.

Howie's idea finally won out. He suggested the boys collect tinfoil and send it to be made into tanks and trucks for the soldiers. "We'll make a ball of tinfoil six feet wide," he said grandly. "We'll

19

roll it up the aisle during the assembly." The boys
were impressed. On the blackboard, Miss Campbell
wrote

*Boys—
Collect Tinfoil for Ball*

When the dismissal bell rang, Miss Campbell
said, "Thank you for working hard today. Good
luck on your projects! Now line up quietly! Where's
your hat, Grace? Put your coat all the way on,
Howie. I'll see you Monday."

Molly led the line of third-graders marching down the stairs and out of the school building into the pale November sunshine. *Knit socks!* she thought. *It's a bad idea, it really is.* Molly didn't think that just because it was Alison's idea, either. She hopped on one foot and then the other, waiting for Linda and Susan. *I won't knit socks,* Molly decided. *I'll think up another project that will win the contest. Then Alison and Miss Campbell will see who has her thinking cap on.*

Molly, Linda, and Susan usually walked home together. On most days, they stopped and played at Molly's house because Mrs. Gilford, the house-keeper, was at home to keep an eye on them. Mrs. McIntire usually did not get home from her job at the Red Cross until dinnertime, and Linda's mother worked in an airplane factory every afternoon.

When the girls got to the back door of Molly's house, Molly flung it open, took a deep breath, and shouted, "Hurray! Bread day!"

Mrs. Gilford replied with three brisk commands: "Come in. Wipe your feet. Sit at the table like ladies."

The kitchen was steamy. It smelled like warm

raisins. Mrs. Gilford stood at the table behind an army of bowls and measuring cups. She nodded to the girls and pointed with the end of her wooden spoon to the three plates on the table in front of them. "There are your sample slices," she said.

On each plate there was a thick, round, brown piece of bread, heavy with fat raisins. "It's round!"said Susan.

"Boston Brown Bread!" replied Mrs. Gilford. "Baked in an old coffee tin. And not a speck of sugar or butter in it!"

Molly picked up her bread and took a bite. "Mmmmm! This is a good one, Mrs. Gilford."

"I like this bread, too," said Linda.

"Me, too," said Susan. "It tastes like Christmas."

"I like the smell," said Molly with her mouth full. "If I had perfume, I'd want it to smell just exactly like this."

"Hmph! You'd probably have all the dogs in the neighborhood following you around," snorted Mrs. Gilford. But Molly could tell she was pleased.

Making bread was one of the things Mrs. Gilford did to help the war effort. Every week she

tried a new bread recipe. Molly, Linda, and Susan were her official testing committee. Out of all the breads Mrs. Gilford had tried so far, only one had not met with everyone's approval. That was "Red Bread" made with tomato juice. Molly and Linda begged Mrs. Gilford never to make it again. But Susan voted for it because it was pink.

Making bread from scratch during wartime was not easy. Mrs. Gilford had to figure out substitutes for some things that were hard to get, like butter and sugar. But Mrs. Gilford rose to the challenge just as her loaves of bread rose high and brown

and delicious. Of all the changes the war had brought to the McIntire household, the only one Molly could absolutely positively say she liked was Mrs. Gilford's homemade bread.

Today Mrs. Gilford had a pamphlet called *How to Bake by the Ration Book* propped up between a milk bottle and a sack of flour. Molly watched Mrs. Gilford sifting some flour through a strainer. She was making a small snowstorm fall right into a bowl on the kitchen table. It looked like fun—you could make a mess but it wouldn't get you into trouble.

"Can I sift it?" she asked Mrs. Gilford.

"*May* I sift it, and no, you may not. Not in your school clothes. You'd be covered all over with flour. Trot upstairs, put on your playclothes, and *then* you may sign up to be a doughboy."

"That would take too much time," said Linda.

"I don't think I'd better," said Molly. "We have to work on our project."

Mrs. Gilford looked up. "What project?"

"Well, there's a Lend-a-Hand Contest at school. We're supposed to do a project to help the war effort. We only have this weekend to do it.

Whoever does the best project wins a prize," explained Molly.

"And what's your project?" asked Mrs. Gilford with interest.

"We don't know yet," said Molly.

"Yes we do," said Susan. She gave Molly a puzzled look. "We're knitting socks, hundreds and hundreds of socks. Just like you do, Mrs. Gilford."

Mrs. Gilford poured milk into a measuring cup. "I see," she said. "Well, good luck to you. You may take another slice of bread if you wish. No crumbs on the floor, please. Come to me if you decide you need knitting needles and yarn."

"Thank you, Mrs. Gilford," the girls said. They each took another slice of bread off the loaf. Then they went outside and walked over to the garage. There was a storage room above the garage, and the girls liked to talk there. It was a private place they used as a clubhouse. They climbed the stairs to the storage room, already nibbling their second slices of bread.

TOP SECRET

The garage was cold, especially compared to the warm kitchen. It was dark, too, because the only light came from the door at one end of the storage room and a window at the other end. The girls couldn't stand up straight except in the very middle of the storage room because the ceiling was sloped just like the sides of a tent.

The storage room smelled of dust, mothballs, and dried-up paper. It was filled with things waiting to be fixed up, thrown out, or needed again. There was a big trunk with one latch broken, boxes full of books and games with pieces missing, a tarnished tennis trophy, a chest of drawers with a mirror on top that made you look green and speckled, a box labeled "Curtains—Too Short," and a roll-top desk with no drawers. Everything looked ghostly because everything was covered with a gray blanket of dust.

The girls had pushed two old love seats together, face-to-face, right under the window. The love seats were not very comfortable because the springs and padding had fallen out of the bottom of them. But they had high, curved backs, so when they were pushed together they made a sort of boat that floated in a dusty sea.

Linda climbed aboard first. "Knitting!" she groaned. "I'm going to be terrible at this project. I *hate* knitting. Everything I ever knitted came out looking like a piece of chewed string."

"Oh, I think knitting is fun," said Susan. "And socks are cute."

"Have you ever knitted a sock?" asked Molly.

"Well, no," said Susan. "But I've seen people do it."

"Yeah, well it's *hard*," said Molly. "I've watched Mrs. Gilford do it. You have to use three needles sometimes, and count stitches, and purl,

*"I'm going to be terrible at this project.
I hate knitting," Linda groaned.*

and turn the heel, and lots of other complicated things."

Susan looked at Molly for a while. "I'll bet you don't like it just because it's Alison's idea," she said. "You're jealous because Alison won the multiplication bee and Miss Campbell gave her the gold badge today, and you did the worst of anybody."

"That's not true!" said Molly.

"It is too!"

"It is not!"

"It is too!"

"Cut it out," said Linda. "It doesn't matter whose idea it is. I still can't knit."

"I think we should do another project," said Molly.

"We can't," said Susan. "All the girls are doing socks. It's our Lend-a-Hand project. Miss Campbell would be mad at us. *Everyone* would be mad at us if we didn't do socks."

"Listen," said Molly. "Those girls are crazy if they think they can each knit even one pair of socks by Monday. They can't possibly do it. The whole third grade will look terrible. They'll be grateful to us if we do another project. Miss Campbell will be proud of us."

Susan was doubtful. "Well, I don't know."

"Look, you want to win the contest, don't you?"

"Yes, but—"

"Well, believe me, there's no way the third grade girls can ever win by knitting socks. It's up to us. We have to do another project and win the contest for the third grade girls." Molly was firm.

"You make it sound so easy to win," said Linda. "What other project can we do that would be so great? Build a fighter plane or something?"

Susan giggled. "We could become spies and go on a mission to steal top secret information from the enemy."

"Hey!" said Molly. "That's it! We sort of *could* be secret agents."

"What do you mean?" asked Susan.

"Well," said Molly, "we're secret agents because nobody knows what we're doing, right? Just us three. And our mission is our project. Only instead of stealing information, we can collect something, something like—"

"Tops! Bottletops!" interrupted Linda. "Get it?

Top Secret. We'll be Top Secret Agents."

"Yes!" said Molly. "That's it! We'll collect bottletops for scrap metal. They use scrap metal to make tanks and battleships and things, so it's good for the war effort. We'll collect at least a hundred bottletops, and we'll surprise everybody in school on Monday. And we'll win the contest, and Miss Campbell will be pleased with us."

"Top Secret Agents!" said Susan. "Just like in the movies. We can wear matching clothes. You know, spy clothes—dark pants and dark shirts—and send notes in a secret code, and have a secret hide-out."

"Right here!" said Molly. "This can be our hide-out."

"We should have a secret handshake, too," said Linda. "And we can never show anybody what it is."

"And we can't tell anybody what our secret project is," said Molly. "We have to be sworn to secrecy."

"Okay, let's swear," said Linda. "Come on! A solemn oath!" She raised her right hand. Molly and

Susan did, too. "I promise never to tell anyone—"

"Shhh!" Molly interrupted. "I hear something!"

"What is it?" asked Susan. "An enemy spy?"

Molly waved to her to be quiet. She crept over to the window. "It's Alison! Alison Hargate is knocking on the kitchen door!"

"I want to see," said Linda. She joined Molly at the window.

"Get down!" Molly commanded. She and Linda knelt by the window.

"Hey, look!" said Linda. "Alison has a big white envelope in her hand."

They looked down at Alison from their hide-out. They saw Mrs. Gilford come to the door, wiping her hands on her apron. Alison showed Mrs. Gilford the envelope. Mrs. Gilford nodded and squinted up at the garage, then pointed right at the window. The girls ducked. They heard footsteps coming toward the garage.

"She's coming this way!" whispered Linda. "She's coming to find us."

"Quick! Hide!" Molly hissed.

"But—" said Susan.

"Hurry *up*," ordered Molly. "If she sees us it

will ruin everything!" She slithered under one of
the love seats. Linda hid behind a trunk. Susan
knelt in a corner, then popped up like a jack-in-the-
box and ran over to hide under the roll-top desk.

Molly's heart was pounding. It smelled musty
under the couch, and the broken springs dug into
her back. After what seemed like a long time, she
heard the door open. All she could see were
Alison's feet. The feet came into the room and
stopped.

"Molly?"

Molly held her breath.

The feet hesitated, then turned and went out the door. Molly could hear them hurrying down the stairs. All her breath came out in one big sigh.

"The coast is clear," she said. Then she wiggled out from under the love seat like a snake going backwards. Linda went back to the window and reported on Alison's movements.

"She's knocking on the door again. Wait! No, she isn't. She's not knocking. She's just . . . she's just leaving the envelope stuck on the doorknob. I guess she's scared to talk to Mrs. Gilford again. Now she's running away, down the driveway." Linda turned away from the window. "She's gone."

"Well, I don't see why we had to hide," huffed Susan. She had dust in her hair and dirt streaked across the back of her coat. "It's only Alison."

"Alison's our friend, but she's not a Top Secret Agent," Molly explained. "If she saw us up here she'd ask what we're doing, and pretty soon our whole secret project wouldn't be secret anymore. It wouldn't be a surprise. It wouldn't be anything at all, and we'd be just like everyone else. Remember, we promised to keep it secret."

"Come on," said Linda. "Let's go! I can't wait

to see what's in that envelope." She was already halfway out the door. Molly and Susan followed close behind into the chill November twilight.

Mrs. Gilford had already turned on the light next to the kitchen door. The girls huddled under it as Molly opened the envelope and pulled out a card. "It's an invitation," she said.

"Ooooooooh! Let me see," said Susan. She stood on tiptoe and leaned over Molly's shoulder.

YOU ARE INVITED TO
A KNITTING
BEE
TO WORK ON YOUR SOCKS
FOR THE LEND-A-HAND
CONTEST FROM NINE-
O-CLOCK TO THREE-O-
CLOCK TOMORROW AT
ALISON'S HOUSE. LUNCH
AND OTHER REFRESHMENTS
TOO! (BRING YOUR OWN
YARN AND NEEDLES.)

Molly's hands were stiff and cold. Susan took the invitation from her and held it under the light. "Gee, I bet that will be fun," she said. "A knitting bee at Alison's house."

"Probably great refreshments, too," said Linda.

"Oh, I don't know," said Molly. "I don't think it will be great. All they'll do is sit and knit, knit and sit all day. I think we'll have more fun collecting bottletops."

"Well, I want to go home and see if I got an invitation, too," said Susan.

"I'm cold," said Linda. "I'm going home, too."

"Okay," said Molly. "Meet back here at nine o'clock sharp tomorrow."

Linda and Susan waved good-bye and hurried off into the gray night. Molly looked at the invitation one more time, then crumpled it up, put it in her coat pocket, and went inside.

SPIES
AND ALLIES

Plip, plop, plip, plop, plip. . . . Molly rolled over in bed and opened her eyes to a weepy, wet day. The windows of her room were blurred like teary eyes. *Oh, no,* she thought. *What a day to be outside, going door to door collecting bottletops!*

Molly got up and put on her spy outfit—dark blue corduroy pants and a dark plaid shirt—and thumped down the stairs to the kitchen.

On cold, rainy Saturdays, Molly's mother always made a warm breakfast. She believed children needed food that would stick to their ribs. Today she made thick, hot oatmeal.

"Why are you wearing that good plaid shirt

today?" Mrs. McIntire asked Molly. "Mrs. Gilford just ironed it. Why don't you save it for school?"

"I need to wear it today, Mom," said Molly, looking down at the shirt. "I'll be careful. We're working on our project."

"What project is that?" Mrs. McIntire asked. She put a bowl of oatmeal in front of Molly and another in front of Ricky. Ricky began pouring honey on top of his oatmeal with one hand, and filling a glass of tomato juice with the other.

"It's for school," said Molly. "Linda and Susan and I are doing a Lend-a-Hand project. Everyone is doing something for the war effort this weekend. There's a contest to see who has the best project."

"Well, that sounds very worthwhile," said Mrs. McIntire.

"Sounds like a dumb elementary school contest to me," said Ricky. He was in the seventh grade. "What are you triple dips going to do, sign up to be monkeys in the zoo?" Ricky pretended his spoon was a banana and began to peel it. "Ooooh, ooh, oooh," he said as he scratched the top of his head like a chimpanzee.

"That's enough, Ricky," said Mrs. McIntire.

"Very funny," said Molly. "*That* wouldn't help win the war. For your information, we have a very good project."

"Yeah? What is it?" Ricky asked.

"I can't tell."

"I can't tell," mimicked Ricky in a high voice. "Well, just don't touch any of *my* stuff." Ricky pointed to himself with the hand that was holding the glass of tomato juice. Some of the juice sloshed over the edge of the glass onto his shirt. Ricky clutched at the red stain. "Oooh, ya got me!" he said. He jerked his head back, closed his eyes, and slumped off the edge of his chair onto the floor. "Dead," he said.

Molly giggled.

"Off with that shirt, young man," Mrs. McIntire said calmly. "That juice will stain if I don't get rid of it right away."

As Ricky took off his shirt, Molly rinsed off her oatmeal bowl at the sink, dried her hands, and went to the closet to get her school bag, raincoat, and hat.

"Boots, too," said Mrs. McIntire without looking up from the sink.

Molly groaned. She didn't think real spies had to wear boots. But she took hers out of the closet and sat on the kitchen floor to put them on.

Molly had not used her boots since last winter, and they were a little dusty. The toe of her saddle shoe went in, but no matter how she yanked and pulled and pushed, her whole shoe would not fit inside her boot. She got up and hip-hopped over to her mother. "Look, Mom," she said. "My boots won't go on over my new saddle shoes. I guess I can't wear boots today."

Mrs. McIntire knelt down and tried to wiggle the boot on to Molly's foot. It would not budge. "Well," she said as she stood up. "You can't wear *these*. They're too small for you now."

"I'll have to get new ones," said Molly. "Maybe I can get red boots this year."

Mrs. McIntire stood up. She fastened the top button on Molly's raincoat. "I'm afraid not, dear," she said. "There are no rubber boots in the stores. I've looked. They're not being made."

"But why?" asked Molly.

"Because of the war," her mother said. "The rubber is needed to make things for the fighting men. Things like life rafts for battleships and life jackets for sailors. There just isn't enough rubber left over to make red rubber boots for nine-year-old girls." Mrs. McIntire leaned into the closet. "You'll have to wear Ricky's boots today." She held up Ricky's old black boots.

"My boots?" said Ricky. "She's going to wear *my* boots?"

"But, Mom," said Molly. "Those are boys' boots. They're ugly. They're—"

"Molly," Mrs. McIntire interrupted. "Think of it as a sacrifice you're making for the war effort." She handed the boots to Molly.

Molly sighed. She took the boots.

"And don't wreck them," said Ricky. "Or get perfume on them or anything."

 Molly and her mother had to laugh. "Don't worry. I won't," Molly said. She pulled on Ricky's boots. They were clumsy, heavy boots with rusted buckles. The buckles fastened up the front, not on the side like girls' boots. They were a little bit too big, so Molly clomped like a horse as she made her way to the door.

"Good-bye, Mom," she said. "I probably won't be home for lunch. We'll be too busy to stop."

"All right," said Mrs. McIntire. "Be careful. Don't go into a stranger's house. Be home by three o'clock."

"Okay," said Molly. She went outside. Linda and Susan were coming up the driveway. Susan waddled like a plump duck under her big red umbrella. "My mother made me wear two sweaters under my raincoat," she complained. "I can hardly move."

"*My* mother wouldn't let me wear my dark shirt," said Linda. "She didn't have time to wash it. She's been working the late shift at the factory."

"And I have to wear these horrible boots of Ricky's," said Molly. "Oh, well, let's get started." She held up her school bag. "I hope this is big enough to hold all the bottletops," she said.

"Can't we take a break?" asked Susan. "I'm so hot."

"I'm so *cold*," said Linda.

"We can't take a break because we haven't started yet," said Molly. "Come on. Real secret agents have to work in the rain all the time."

There were seven houses on Molly's block. The girls trudged up to each one, rang the doorbell, and asked for bottletops.

At the first house, Mrs. Silvano said she didn't have any bottletops, but did they want old newspapers? They said no, thank you very much.

Billy Ruckstein answered the door at the next house. He was only four. He said yes, they did have bottletops. Then he ran off and came back with a top still connected to a whole bottle of ginger ale. The girls told him the top had to be off the bottle already, but thanked him very much.

They walked on to the Koloskis' house. Mr. Koloski said he had two bottletops, but he needed them himself. He was a Boy Scout troop leader, and the Boy Scouts were collecting bottletops for scrap metal, too.

Finally, Mrs. Keller gave them six bottletops she

had been saving but had never gotten around to turning in. And Mrs. Leaming gave them four. She said if they wanted more they should come back next Saturday, because she was having a party then and she'd have lots of bottletops after the party.

By the time they'd gone to all seven houses on the block they had cold hands, wet legs, tired feet, and ten bottletops in Molly's school bag.

"Let's count them," said Susan. She handed her umbrella to Linda.

"What for?" said Linda. "We know perfectly well there are only ten."

"I know, but I want to see them," said Susan. She dug her hands into the school bag and pulled out two handfuls. Molly and Linda watched as she dropped the bottletops into the bag one by one. "One, two, three, four, five, six, seven, eight, nine, ten," she said as they clinked against each other. "I didn't think it would be so hard to get a hundred."

"We'll just have to keep trying," said Molly. "We can't give up now. Let's go to the next block."

Bottletops were scarce on the next block, too. No one was home at two houses. At one house, a

44

*"I didn't think it would
be so hard to get a hundred,"* said Susan.

man came to the door in a painter's hat. He was spattered all over with blue paint. He said if he *did* have any bottletops he'd never be able to find them because the whole house was torn up and in a mess. The girls peeked past him to see if that was true. It was.

One nice lady holding a baby gave them two apple juice bottletops and let them shake hands with the baby. A smiling old lady said they were sweet girls and gave them each one bottletop. As they left, Molly noticed two blue stars hung in her window. "She has *two* people from her family fighting in the war," Molly said.

"We have one blue star for my father," said Linda. "The people next door have a gold star because their son got killed." Molly looked back at the old lady's house. It seemed to be waiting for happy, noisy young people to come back and fill it with fun again.

At the next house, a teen-age boy holding half a chicken sandwich pulled a bottletop out of his pocket, handed it to Molly, and closed the door without saying a word. "Did you see that sandwich?" asked Linda as they headed down the walk.

"I'm hungry. It's lunchtime. We have to stop now."

"Not yet," said Molly. "We only have sixteen bottletops."

"I'm tired," said Susan. "I can't go on any longer."

"Some secret agents *you* two make," said Molly. Her nose was runny. Ricky's boots were heavy. "Come on. Just one more block, then we'll take a break for lunch."

Susan sighed. Linda shivered. Molly led the way across the street to the next block.

"Hey, you know who lives on this block?" Linda asked. "Alison Hargate."

"I know," said Molly. "We just won't go to her house to ask for bottletops."

"I bet Alison has lots of bottletops," said Susan. The girls were now standing right in front of Alison's house.

"I know what! Let's go peek in the window at the knitting bee," said Linda. "It'll be fun! Just like real secret agents!"

"Yes!" said Susan. "Let's spy on them."

Molly hesitated. "What if someone sees us?" she asked. But Linda was already bent over, creeping behind a tall bush and heading toward a big window. Susan put her umbrella in the bush and followed Linda. Finally Molly went, too. She felt out of place standing on the sidewalk all alone.

When she bent over to sneak behind the bushes, the rain dripped down the back of Molly's neck. It gave her goosebumps. Linda and Susan were on tiptoe, holding on to the window ledge, peering inside. Molly looked, too.

Oh, it was so warm and cozy in there! They were looking into Alison's living room, where a cheery fire blazed in the fireplace. All the other girls in their class were sitting Indian-style in a circle on the rug. They had bright balls of yarn in their laps and long slender knitting needles in their hands. The Hargates' maid knelt behind Grace Littlefield, her big capable hands guiding Grace's on the needles. Alison was laughing, and all the other girls looked happy.

"Look at that tray of sandwiches!" said Linda. "And cocoa and cookies, too!"

"It looks like fun," said Susan wistfully. "The yarn is pretty."

"I don't see any socks," said Molly.

"Look, Grace can't even hold her needles right," giggled Linda.

"WELL! What have we here?" boomed a voice very close by. The girls jumped.

It was Mrs. Hargate, Alison's mother! She was standing right behind them, blocking their path back to the sidewalk, holding a big black umbrella. Drips from the umbrella hit Molly right on the cheek. Mrs. Hargate had on very red lipstick.

"You girls are late for the knitting bee," said Mrs. Hargate. "But that doesn't matter. Come along! Alison was *so* worried when you didn't get here at nine with all the other gals. She was afraid you weren't coming *at all*. But I told her that you'd *never* be so rude. You'd never miss out on all the fun and not help on the project. I said I was sure you'd turn up, and I was right. Here you are!" Mrs. Hargate kept talking as she herded them inside like captured criminals. Linda, Molly, and Susan didn't have time to say anything. Molly didn't know what to say, anyway.

Before they knew it, the three girls were standing in the Hargates' front hall, the water dripping off their coats and forming a small puddle

"WELL! What have we here?"
boomed a voice very close by.

around them. "Look who *I* found," Mrs. Hargate called to Alison in a very loud voice as she took off her coat. "Darling Linda, Susan, and Molly were waiting outside! Take off those sopping coats, girls. And the boots, too. Why, Molly, aren't those boots a teensy bit too big for you? Scoot along now. Go on in and join the party. I'll be in the den if you need me."

Molly, Linda, and Susan bumped into one another, each trying to be the last one to enter the living room. Alison jumped up from the circle and said, "Hi."

"Hi," mumbled Linda, Susan, and Molly.

"We were afraid you weren't coming," said Alison. "Where are your knitting needles and yarn?" She looked behind them, as if they might be hiding yarn and needles there as a surprise.

"We don't have any," said Linda.

"Oh, well, it doesn't matter," said Alison. "I have lots of extra needles, and none of us has used very much yarn yet. Sit down, and I'll get everything for you."

Molly, Linda, and Susan sat awkwardly on the edge of the couch behind the circle of knitters. They

 looked like three crows on a branch.
"Here," Alison said as she handed
them needles and yarn. "I hope the
colors are okay. And I hope you're good knitters.
We sure need some. How come you were so late?"

Linda looked at Molly. Molly looked at Susan.
Susan twisted a strand of yarn around her finger.
"Well," she said, "we're not doing knitting. I mean,
we have another project. We're—"

Molly jabbed Susan with her elbow and Susan
stopped talking.

Alison looked puzzled. "You're not making
socks? You have *another* Lend-a-Hand project?"

Molly took a deep breath. "We're sort of just
visiting you. We're doing a different project."

"What is it?" asked Alison.

"It's a secret," said Molly.

"Oh." Alison went back to knitting. Molly,
Linda, and Susan just watched. The other girls
knitted silently.

Molly noticed that none of the knitters had
gotten very far. Most of the girls had knitted only
the top part of one sock. They were just getting to
the hard part, the heel, where they needed to use

three needles. What they had knitted didn't look at all like socks. They had knitted squares about the size of a doll's blanket.

A blanket! Molly sat up on the edge of the couch. That's what they should knit, not socks! They could knit squares, then sew them together to make a big blanket. They practically had enough squares already. A blanket was such a good idea! So much easier than socks! So much faster! But Molly didn't dare say anything. After all, it wasn't *her* project.

Suddenly, Grace Littlefield threw down her needles. She looked ready to cry. Everyone stared at her. "I can't do this," she wailed. "I just can't! It was hard enough with the two needles, but three is impossible! Every stitch I knit comes undone. I'll never make a whole sock, never!"

Molly felt sorry for Grace. She slid off the couch and sat on the floor next to her. "Socks are hard, Grace," she said. "But you know, you have a nice square here. If we—I mean, if *you*—all put your squares together, you could make a really nice blanket. I saw Mrs. Gilford do it once. See, you just lay out the squares. . . ."

"We're making *socks*," said Alison.

Molly sat back up on the couch.

"Wait a minute," said one of the other girls. "Maybe Molly has a good idea. We all have squares already. If we all make just one or two more, we could make a big blanket."

"But how do we sew the squares together?" asked Alison.

"Oh, I know how to do *that*," said Linda. "You don't have to be able to knit to do *that*. You just need a big sewing needle."

"Oh, let's try it," said Grace. "A blanket is a good idea."

Molly jumped up. "We should have an assembly line," she said. "The best knitters keep knitting. Grace, you collect the squares and flatten them out. Linda, you and I will sew the squares together."

"I'll finish your square, Grace," said Susan.

"I'll go find a big sewing needle," said Alison.

All of a sudden, everyone was talking at once. The knitters clicked away on their needles, finishing square after square. Grace hurried from knitter to knitter, collecting, flattening, and organizing the finished squares. Molly and Linda sat up on the couch. Linda sewed the brightly colored squares together into long strips. Molly sewed the strips together. Slowly, the knitted blanket grew until Molly had to drape it over the back of the couch. Finally, the needles were still.

All of the girls stood up and lifted the blanket to fold it. Susan held one edge up to her cheek. "I think this is the most beautiful blanket anyone ever made in the whole world."

"And we all did it. I don't even remember which squares I made now that they're all together," said Alison.

"But do you think a blanket can win the Lend-a-Hand Contest?" asked Mary Lou Dobbs. "Is a blanket a good war effort?"

"Oh, *yes*," said Molly. Her fingers were sore where she had pricked them with the needle, and her legs were stiff from sitting still so long. "Just this week we got a letter from my dad saying that they really need blankets in the hospitals. It gets pretty cold in England, and winter is coming soon."

"Just think!" said Alison. "This blanket may keep some poor wounded soldier warm."

*Slowly, the knitted blanket grew until
Molly had to drape it over the back of the couch.*

"It may save his life," Linda added.

All the girls looked at the blanket again.

"I'm *sure* it will win the prize," said Molly.

The girls folded the blanket as carefully as if it

 were a flag. "I'll wrap it in paper so it won't get dirty on the way to school," said Alison. She turned to Molly. "A blanket was a good idea, Molly. We couldn't have done it without you. Are you sure. . . . I mean, what about your other project? Could we all help you with that?"

Molly looked down at her feet. "It isn't such a great project," she said. "Not like the blanket."

"And we weren't doing too well, anyway," said Linda.

"What was it?" asked Grace.

Susan, Molly, and Linda looked at each other. They all smiled.

"Oh, it was *terrible*," said Susan. "We were collecting bottletops for scrap metal, and we knocked on everybody's door. It was so hard. We only got sixteen, and then we decided to come over here and sp— I mean, come over and see what you were doing."

"Collecting bottletops is a good project," said Alison. "I'll go ask my mother if she has any."

"If we all ask our mothers, we can get pretty many," said another girl.

"We wanted to get one hundred," said Linda.

"You know what?" said Grace. Her face was shiny and excited. "I live in an apartment building. There are twenty families in my building. We can ask all of them. I bet we'll get a hundred bottletops easily!"

"Yes, and we won't get wet!" laughed Molly. "Let's go!"

"We only need seventy-eight more," said Alison. "My mother had six!" She put the bottle-tops in Molly's school bag.

Molly smiled at her. "Thanks, Alison!" she said. Alison smiled, too.

With a flurry of buckling, zipping, buttoning, and tying, the ten girls got into their raincoats, boots, and rain hats. They set off for Grace's apartment building. As they splashed down the wet street, laughing and talking and planning, Molly decided that some secrets are a lot more fun when you give them away than when you keep them.

JEFFERSON DAILY NEWS

Molly McIntire and her teacher, Miss Charlotte Campbell, with winning project.

THIRD GRADE GIRLS WIN LEND-A-HAND CONTEST

Ten students at Willow Street School showed the true meaning of allied effort this weekend. The third-grade girls won first prize in the school's contest to help the war effort. They knitted a blanket and collected 100 bottletops, which they made into a sign saying "Lend A Hand."

"Both projects were a surprise to me," said their teacher. "I don't know how the girls managed to finish them in one day. I am very proud of every one of the girls." At a school assembly today, each girl was given a blue ribbon.

The blanket will be sent to a hospital in England, where Dr. James McIntire, the father of Molly McIntire, is working with the U.S. Army Medical Corps. The bottletops will be given to the Boy Scouts' scrap metal drive.

This article appeared in Molly's hometown newspaper.

LOOKING
BACK
1944

A PEEK INTO
THE PAST

SCHOOL IN 1944

Molly and her classmates studied many of the same subjects you do today, but their school was different from yours. In 1944 most children walked or rode their bikes to a school in their own neighborhood. Often the school was so nearby that children could go home for lunch and come back for afternoon classes. Teachers like Miss Campbell were usually stricter than teachers are today, and classrooms were quieter and more orderly. The desks and chairs in classrooms like Molly's were often fastened to the floor in straight rows. At recess time, students marched in and out of the building in neat, orderly lines. There were often separate playgrounds for boys and girls. Sometimes boys and girls even had separate doors they used to go in and out of the school building.

If you went to school with Molly, you'd start every day by saluting the flag and singing a song like "America the Beautiful" or "The Star Spangled Banner." During World War Two, American children were taught to be patriotic and proud supporters of their country's war effort. Besides reading, spelling, arithmetic, and geography, they studied the war nearly every day in school. They learned why the United States was fighting Japan and Germany, and they studied the countries where their fathers, brothers, uncles, and friends were soldiers. They marked maps to keep track of the places where American troops were fighting.

American students also studied what it was like for children to live in Europe, China, and the Pacific Islands—places where the fighting was going on. They

Children being evacuated from London

sometimes wrote letters to pen pals in England. Children from cities like London wrote back about being *evacuated*—moving to the countryside and living with friends, relatives, or even strangers whose homes were safe from German bombs. Studying children in other countries helped American students understand how lucky they were to be far away from the fighting.

Teachers also explained why a faraway war made things scarce on America's home front. Some things, like

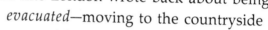

Student marking map

64

sugar and rubber, were scarce because the war was going on in the countries where sugar and rubber came from. Things made of metal were hard to get because most of the metal was being used to make airplanes, tanks, ships, and military trucks. In the United States, many scarce things were *rationed* during the war. This meant Americans could buy only small amounts of them.

Students also learned to do their part to help their country win the war. Every school had scrap drives

Scrap drives

Children with a knitted blanket

and contests like the Lend-A-Hand Contest at Molly's school. In scrap drives, children collected old pots and pans, paper, foil, cans, and car tires that could be used to make war equipment. Children also belonged to the Junior Red Cross, the Scouts, and church groups. These groups made food packages for soldiers, rolled bandages out of strips of cloth, and knitted sweaters, socks, and blankets for the fighting men.

Students used their allowances to support America's war effort, too. They bought War Stamps. War Stamps cost 25 cents each. Some children bought over $100 worth of War Stamps in a year. Money from these stamps was used to buy war equipment.

During the war, children like Molly had less money to spend than you do today. When they bought War Stamps, they did not have very much money left for toys, treats, or extras of any kind. In school, they learned how to take care of their books, clothes, and other belongings to make them last longer. They tried to be cooperative, responsible citizens. They believed what Miss Campbell said to her third grade class: "School is your war duty. Being a good student is as important as being a good soldier."

WAR MESSAGE
to children

Our country is at war. From the Philippines to Iceland your brothers, uncles, and friends in our armed forces are on guard. Our President has told us that the war may be long. Each of you and each of your teachers has a job to do. In this message I am going to try to tell you what that job is.

- **First,** be sure that you know what we are fighting for.
- **Second,** love your country more than ever before.
- **Third,** it is your job to keep calm.
- **Fourth,** part of your job is to help with war work. Save your money. Buy defense stamps. Learn to save paper and pencils and books. Learn to do without things so that the work of our men will go to help our army and navy and our friends in other countries.
- **Fifth,** do today's work well. Your work in school is to study and to learn. You must learn from books but you must also learn to work and to play with other pupils and with your teachers. When peace comes, you will be stronger if you have done today's job well.

From a wartime magazine